W9-CFB-302

Nicholas Allan

A Doubleday Book for Young Readers

To Viktor and Diemüt

A Doubleday Book for Young Readers

Published by
Bantam Doubleday Dell Publishing Group, Inc.
1540 Broadway
New York, New York 10036

First American Edition 1998

Originally published in Great Britain by Hutchinson Children's Books,
a division of Random House UK Ltd., 1997.

Library of Congress Cataloging-in-Publication Data

ISBN 0-385-32573-8
Cataloging-in-Publication Data is available from the U.S. Library of Congress.

The text of this book is set in 14-point Stempel Garamond.

Printed in Singapore

April 1998

10 9 8 7 6 5 4 3 2 1

There were no animals or people on the island, so the hermit had it all to himself . . . which was just how he liked it.

It was always quiet . . .

. . . always tidy . . .

. . . always peaceful.

But one day . . .

. . . he had a visitor.

Soon it wasn't quiet . . .

. . . or tidy . . .

. . . or peaceful.

“This is my island,” said the hermit. “Go find your own.”
“There are no other islands,” said the bird.

So they had to share.
But the hermit didn't like sharing. He wanted his own piece of the island.
"We'll divide the island in two," he said.

So they tried it, and it worked . . .

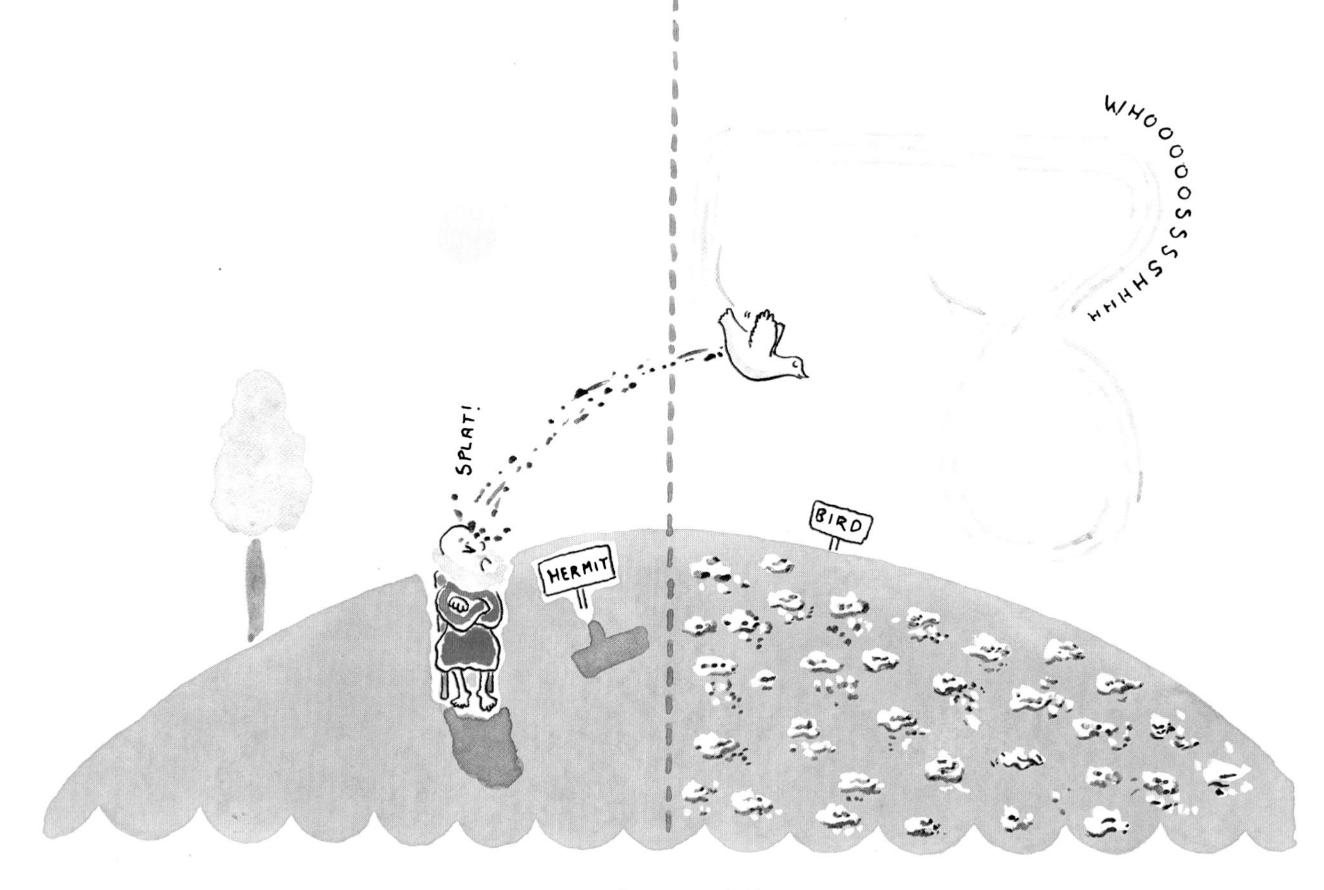

. . . for a while.

Finally, the hermit built a wall.

But it was no good.

The bird had to go.

The hermit
built a trap . . .

. . . and then he
built a cage . . .

. . . and then he made a hood to put over the cage, until . . .
at last . . . there was silence.

He cleaned up the island, lay in the sun, and listened to the silence.

But after a while, the silence bothered him. He even missed the bird's song.

“Please sing,” said the hermit.
But the bird wouldn’t.

“Please make a splat,” said the hermit.
But the bird wouldn’t.

"Please don't fly away," said the hermit.
But the bird did.

Now it was very quiet. The hermit grew lonelier and lonelier, and wished the bird

would come back. He waited and waited for days and nights, until . . . at last . . .

FLAP
FLAP

WHOOOOSSSSHHH
SPLAT!

“Oh, it’s so nice to share with a friend,” said the hermit.
“Yes. There’s nothing like sharing with a friend,” agreed the bird.
“In fact, that’s why I went back to get the others.”
“Others?” said the hermit.

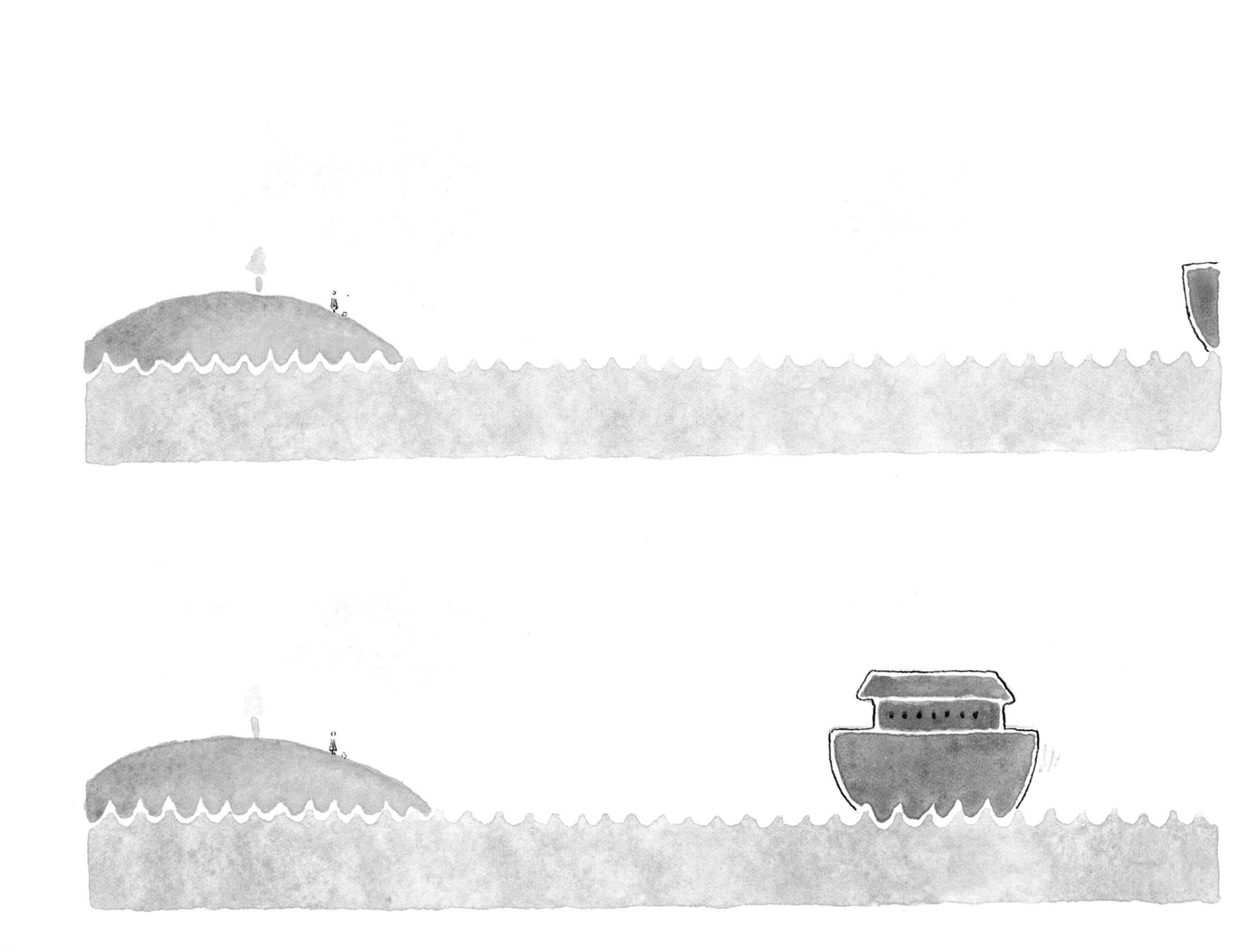

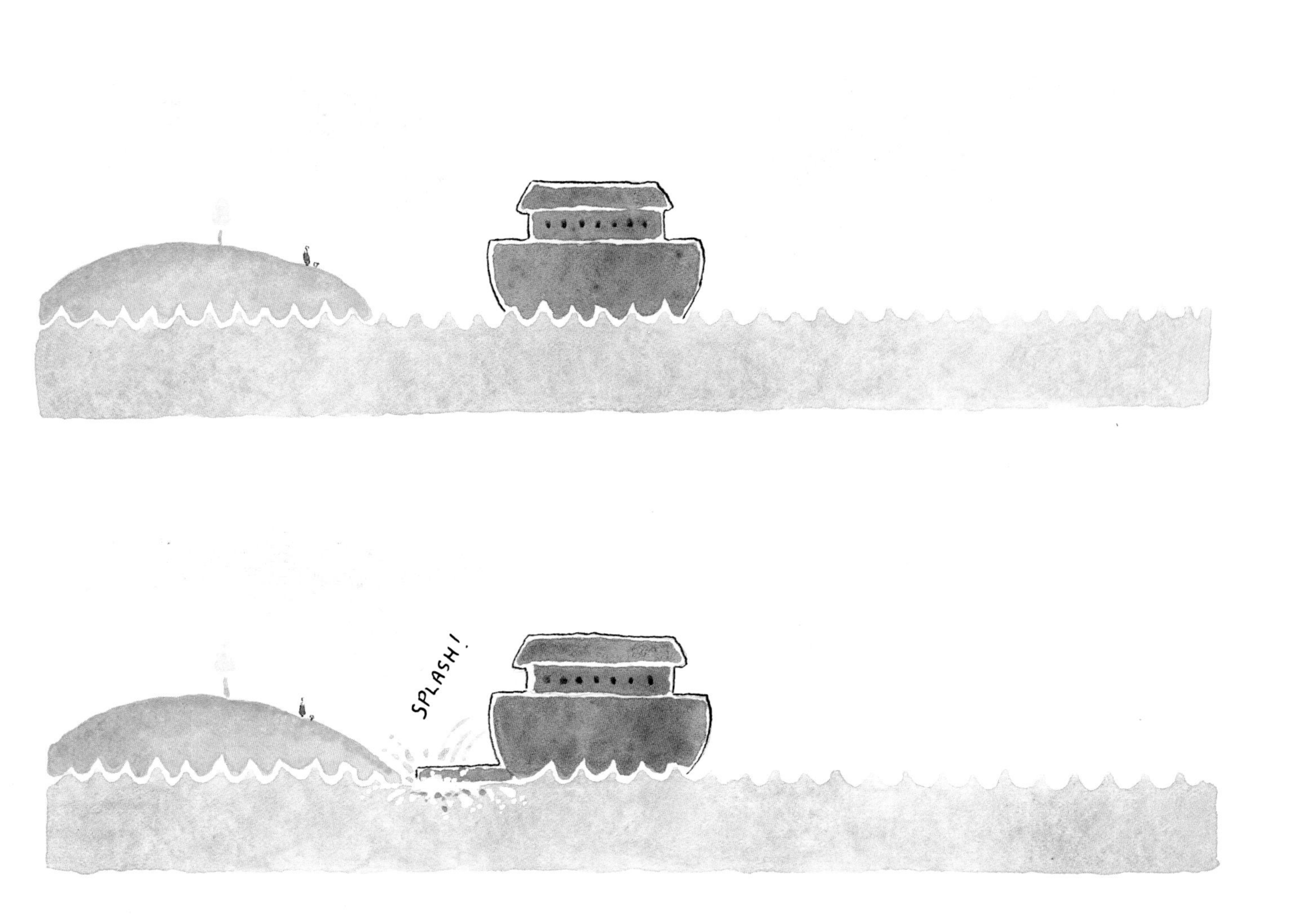
SPLASH!

Mooo!
Mooo!
Baa!
Baa!
Quack!
Quack!
Oink!
Oink
Squeak!
Squeak!

Woof!
Woof!
Roar!
Roar!
Hiss!
Hiss!

"Yes, the others . . ."

Quack!
Quack!
Oink!
Oink!
Woof!
Woof!
Baa!
Baa!

. . . said the Dove.